Witold Generowicz

THE ESCAPE OF THE Kr

To Karen

Viking Kestrel
Penguin Books Australia Ltd,
487 Maroondah Highway, P.O. Box 257
Ringwood, Victoria, 3134, Australia
Penguin Books Ltd,
Harmondsworth, Middlesex, England
Viking Penguin Inc.,
40 West 23rd Street, New York, N.Y. 10010, U.S.A.
Penguin Books Canada Ltd,
2801 John Street, Markham, Ontario, Canada, L3R 1B4
Penguin Books (N.Z.) Ltd,
182-190 Wairau Road, Auckland 10, New Zealand

First published 1987 by Viking

ISBN 0670 80102 X

Made and printed in Hong Kong by Colorcraft Ltd

Witold Generowicz

THE ESCAPE OF THE KroLLsnork

A chase through an amazing fantasy land,
that unfolds into one of the longest books in
the world.

Viking Kestrel

Captured by a circus, the rare and mighty
Krollsnork is taken to a secret place in the
desert, where the circus folk are secretly
testing a weird new building machine.

As the train pulls to a stop, the Krollsnork
makes his move . . .

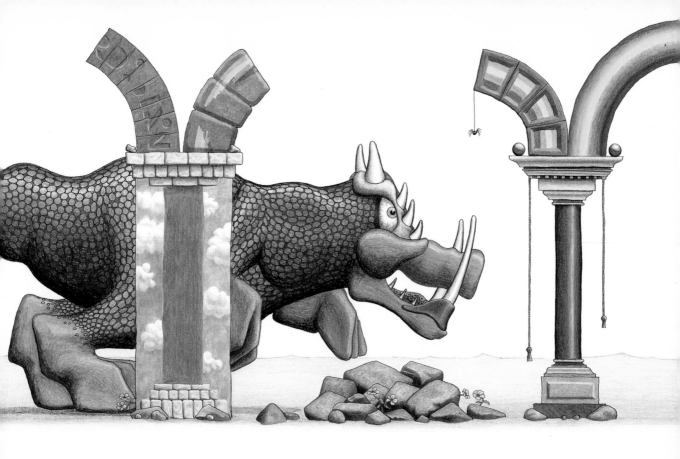

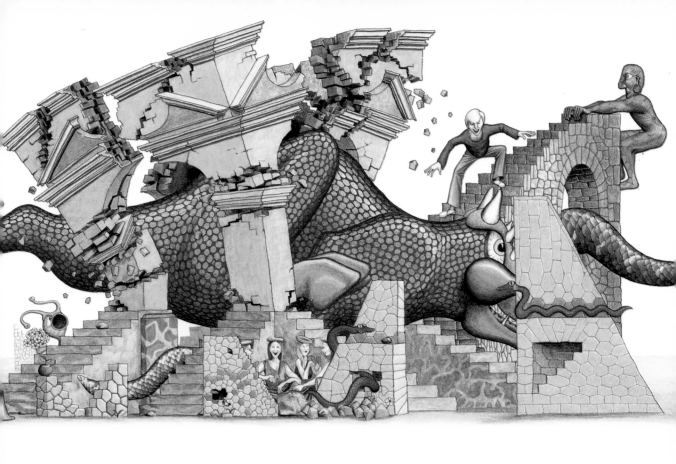

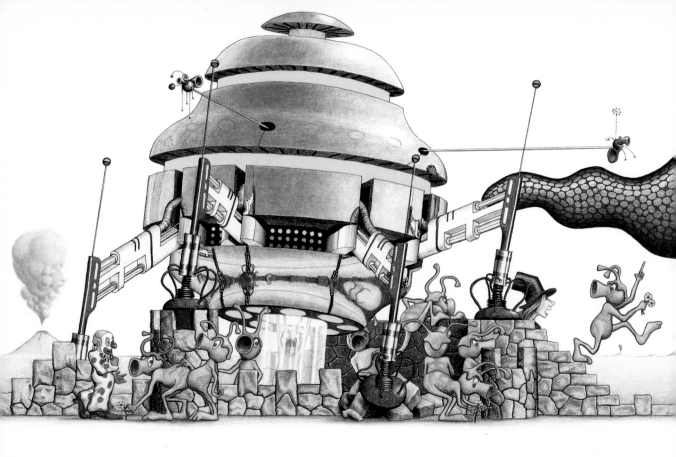

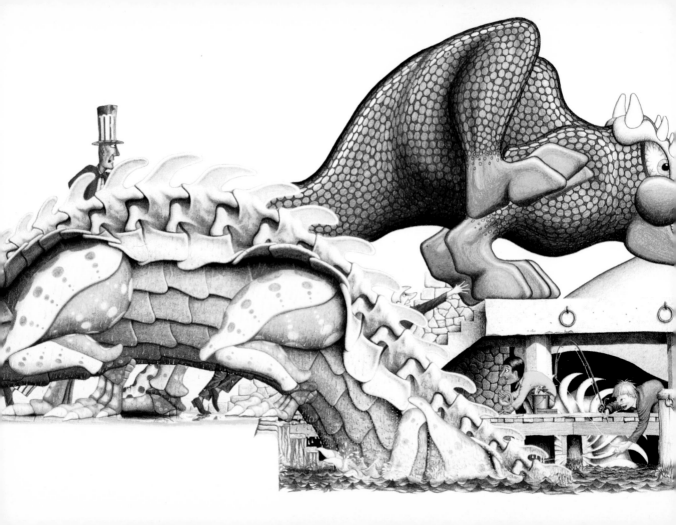

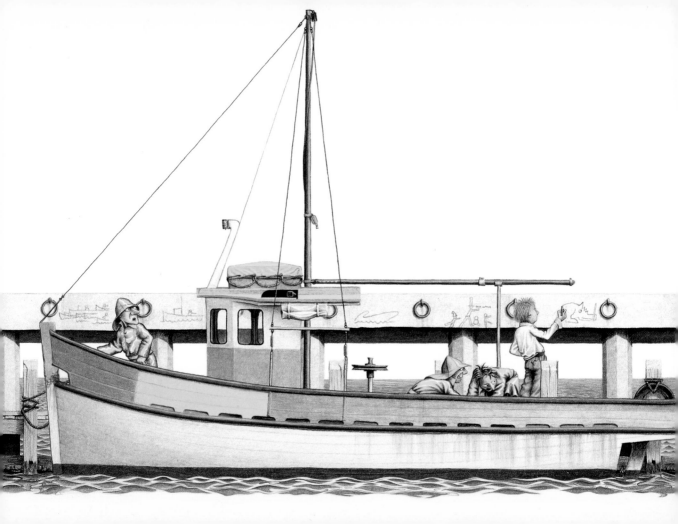

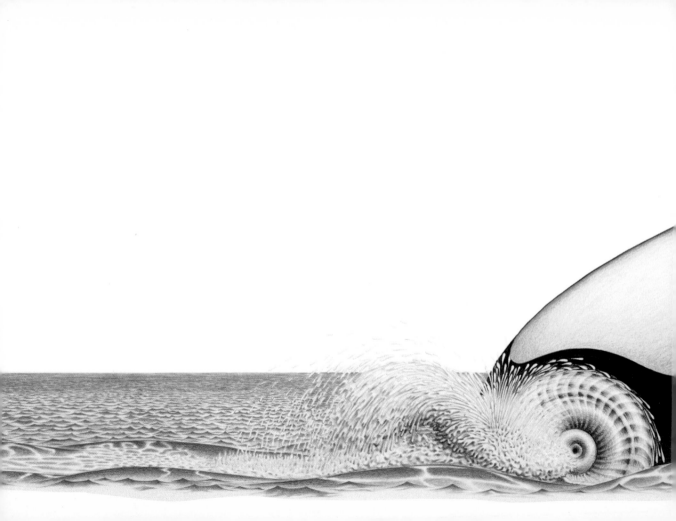